WORDS

CHRISTOPH NIEMANN

GREENWILLOW BOOKS
An Imprint of HarperCollinsPublishers

What can you do with a word?

For me drawing and writing are very closely related. Both a word and a picture have the power to express extremely complex thoughts and emotions with amazing simplicity. Think of the word "love," or a drawing of a smiling face. Being able to understand words and images opens the door to knowledge, communication, and connection to people all over the world.

One of the biggest differences between a word and an image is that most of us learn to understand images through happenstance or playful discovery, whereas learning to read and write usually requires a conscious effort. My aim for this book was to make the discovery of words equally fun and inspiring. By showing words in the context of simple visual scenes, I am inviting kids (and readers of all ages) to intuit and puzzle out meaning, and to see language as a source of ideas and stories.

Browse the pages to discover words you don't know (or find a new facet of the ones you do)! Create your own stories or poems by combining words, images, and ideas. Think of other words to describe the images, or new drawings to interpret the words. Cover a word with your finger and ask a friend to guess it just by looking at the picture. Or pick a word and draw (or write) what you think happens next . . .

I hope *Words* will help you celebrate language and art—at home, at school, in the car, on a plane. Have fun!

—C. N.

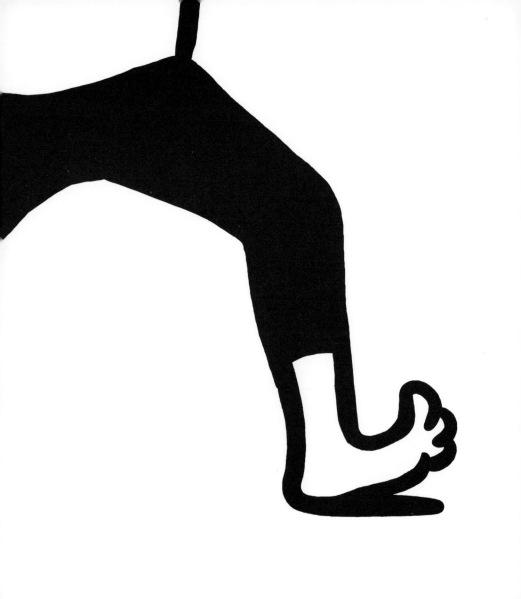

go

put

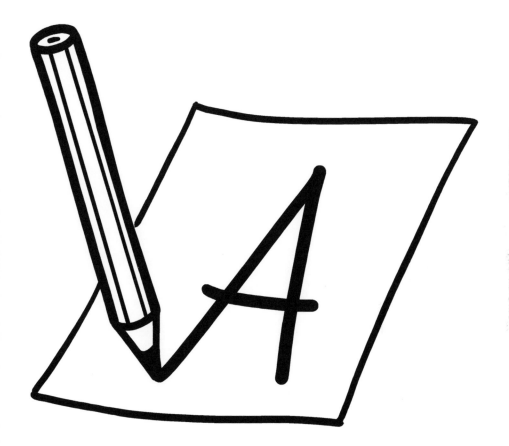

write

search

think

start

stop

love

almost

duck

duck

until

will

must

change

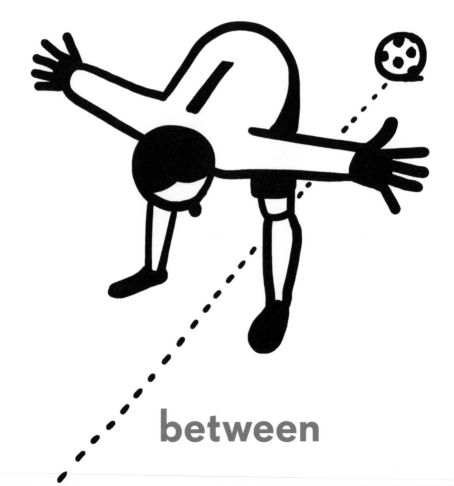

between

us

only

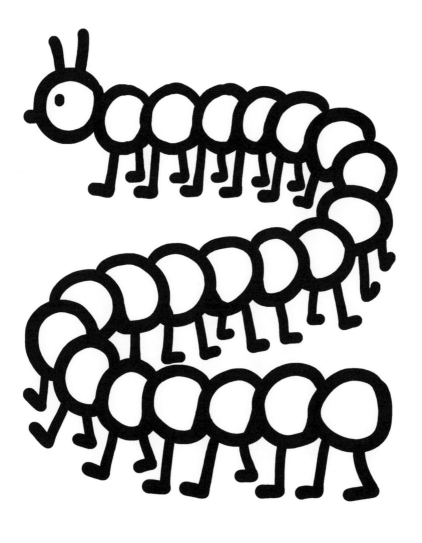

many

most

together

SO

no

do

don't

could

would

what

good

can

hope

my

song

hear

bad

later

but

enough

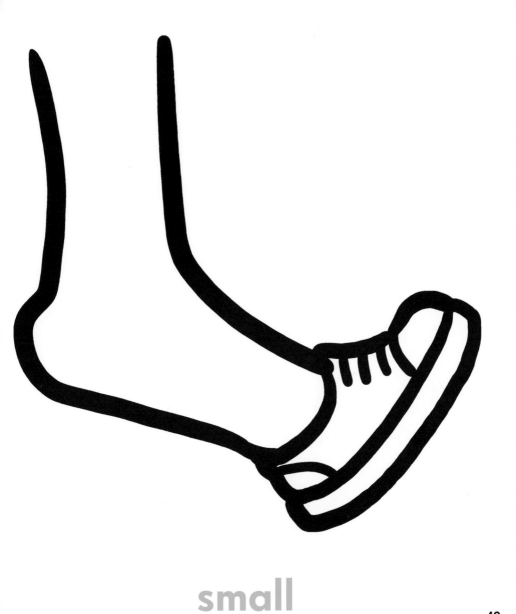

small

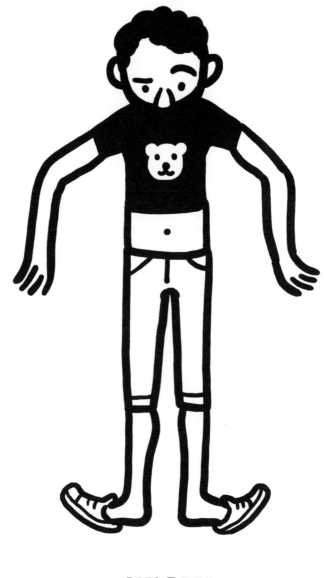

grow

large

real

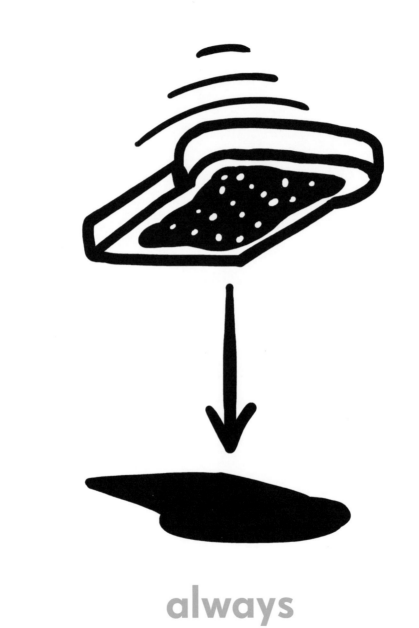

always

miss

on

note

note

left

right

dog

bird

ship

car

street

house

city

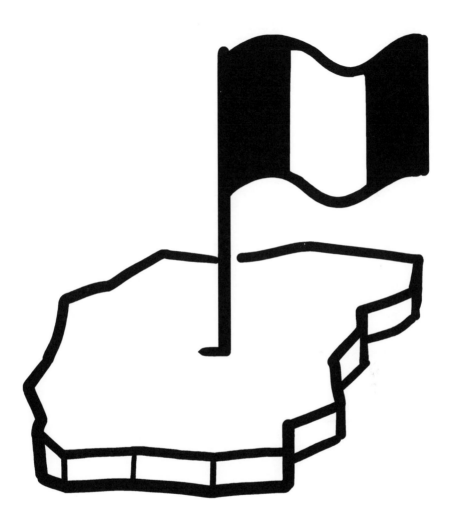

country

world

sky

home

them

lickety-split

wonky

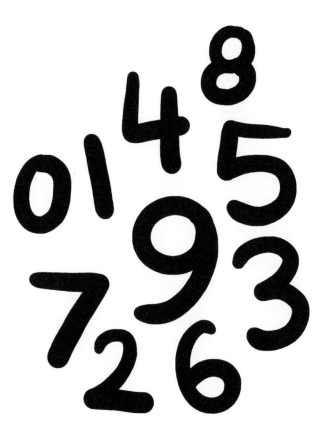

number

one

two

three

four

five

few

half

last

did

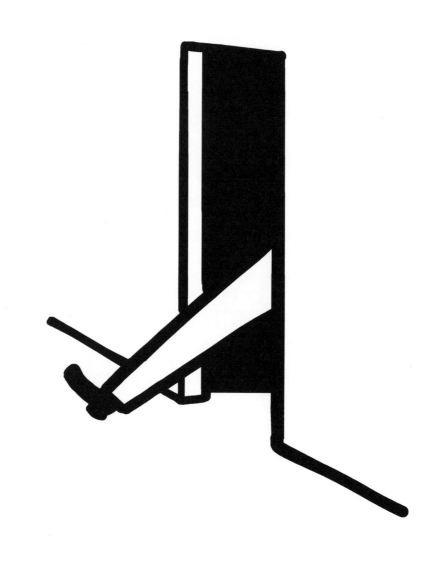

come

here

help

him

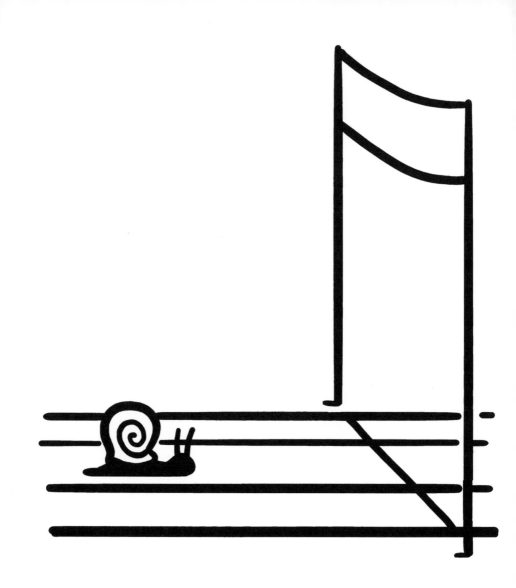

slowly

turn

around

again

again

again

bowl

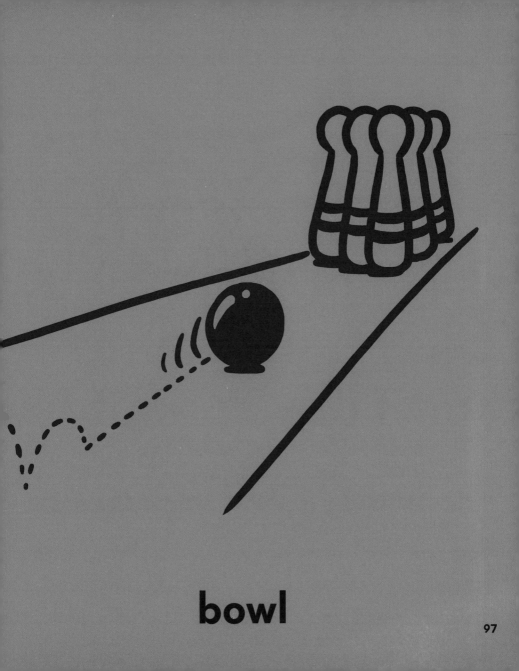

bowl

see

where

there

those

little

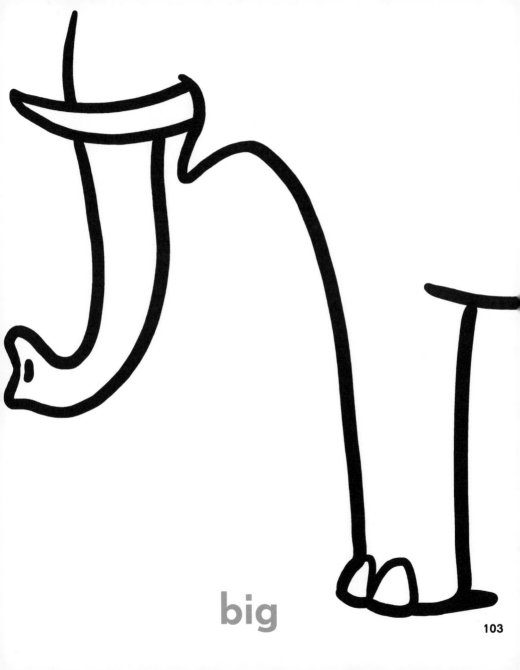

big

as

sea

river

tree

been

still

long

long

watch

if

something

of

that

other

in

out

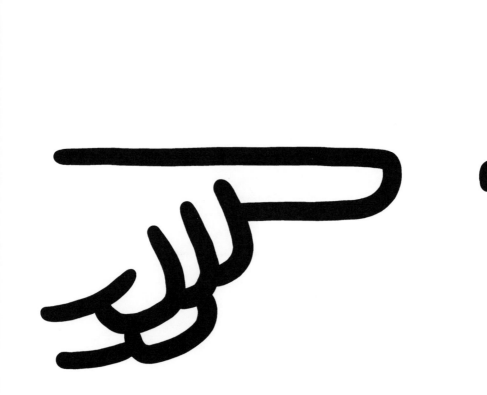

point

press

stick

stick

cat

spell

want

example

this

for

have

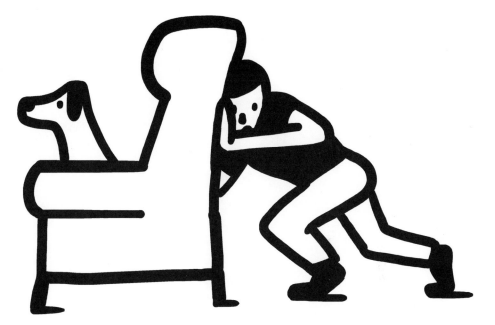

move

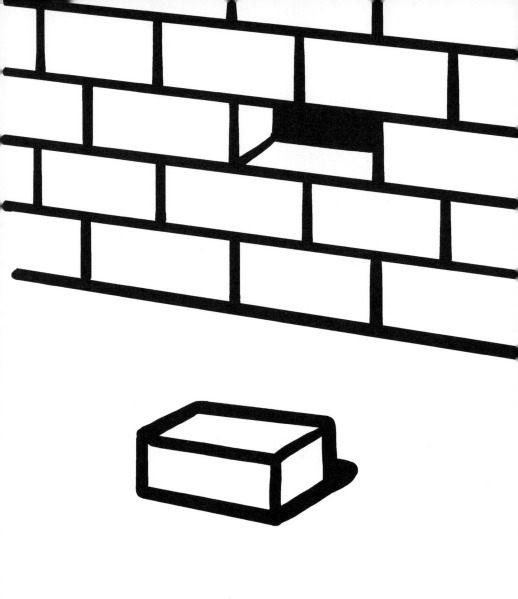

part

group

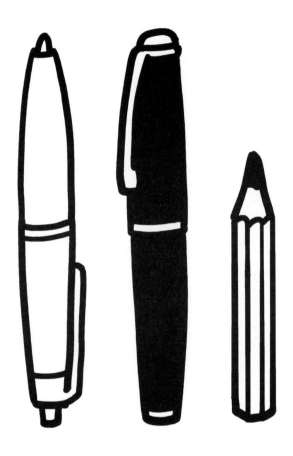

family

farm

eat

test

might

up

horse

rest

share

more

luck

mother

match

match

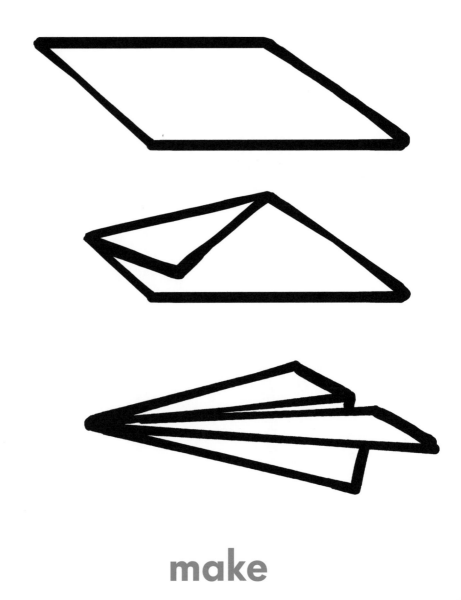

make

carry

took

our

when

never

any

day

night

light

water

Earth

dollop

festooned

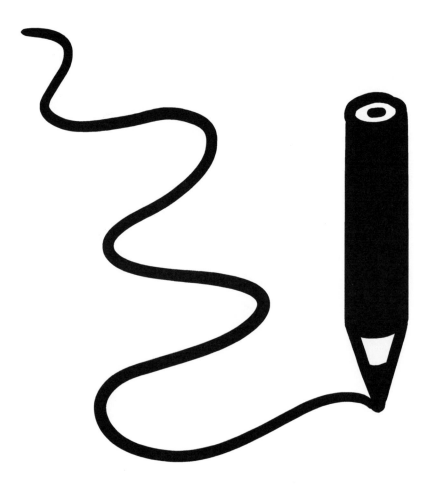

line

cut

from

into

and

at

heavy

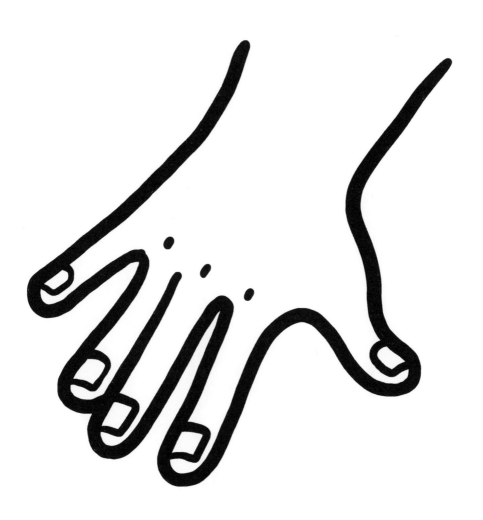

hand

head

feet

finger

close

show

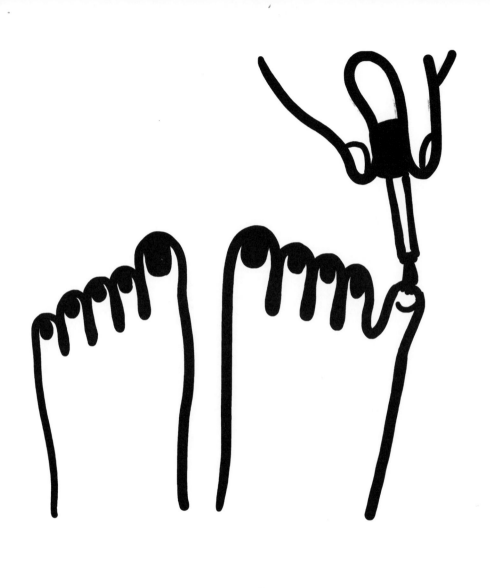

each

new

well

flat

flat

who

they

all

went

by

along

far away

next

another

year

answer

own

open

air

was

leave

lollygag

somnambulist

a

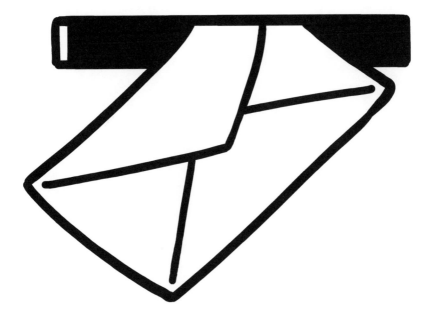

letter

tell

thought

idea

great

school

book

has

run

life

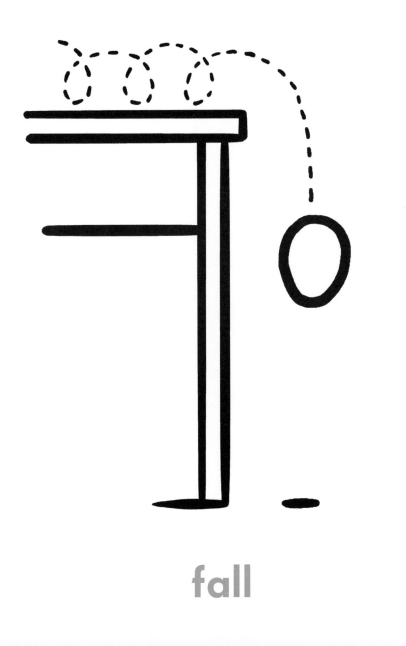

fall

got

need

read

full

begin

then

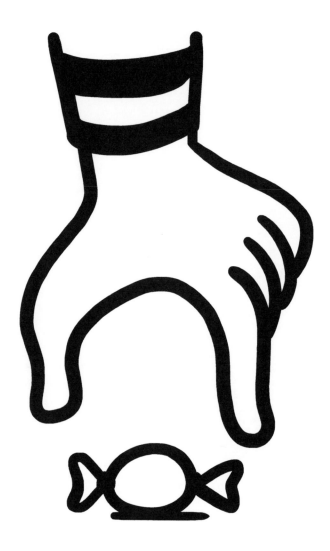

take

thing

keep

fond

set

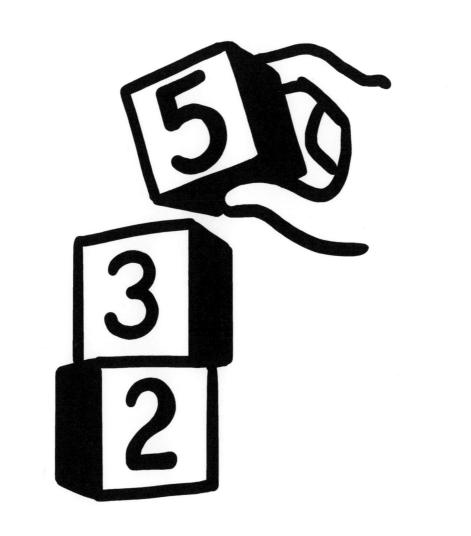

add

follow

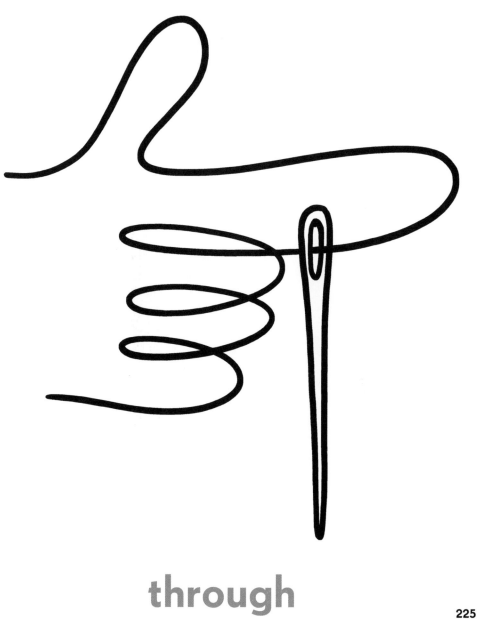

through

over

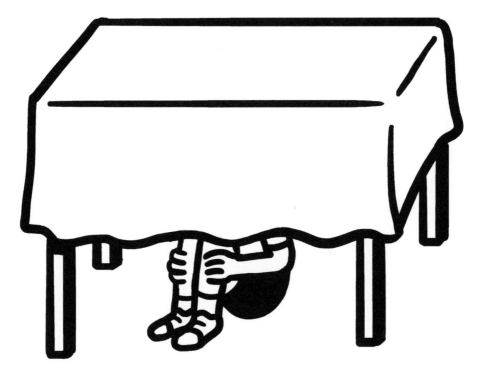

under

above

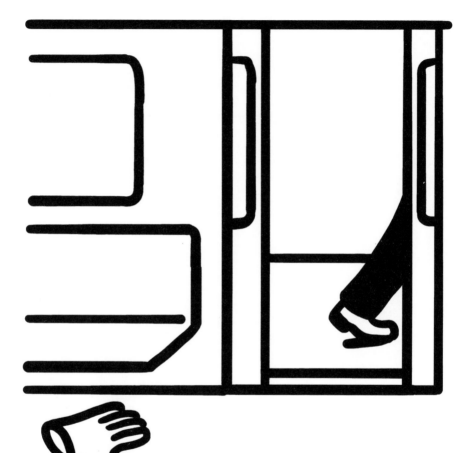

lost

find

me

too

lean

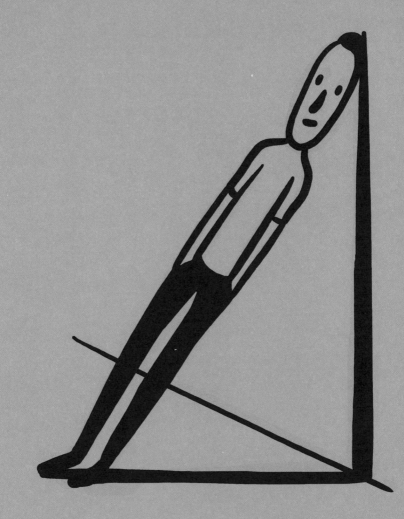

lean

he

old

white

down

side

way   to

mountain

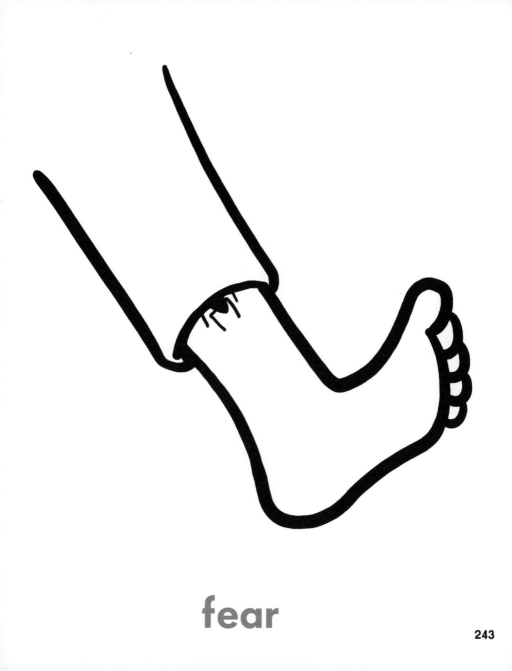

fear

had

said

state

pattern

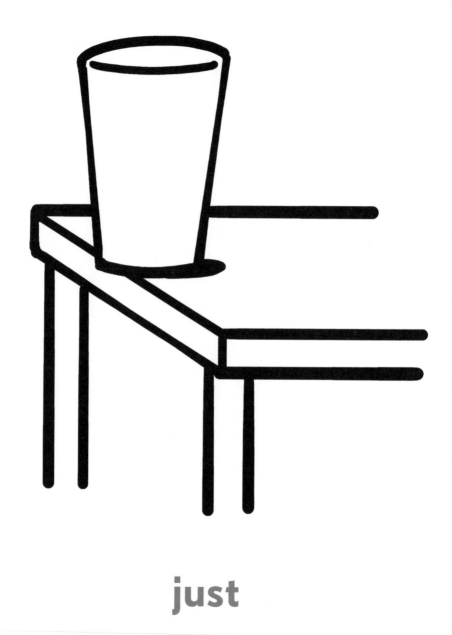

just

not

talk

without

is

very

hard

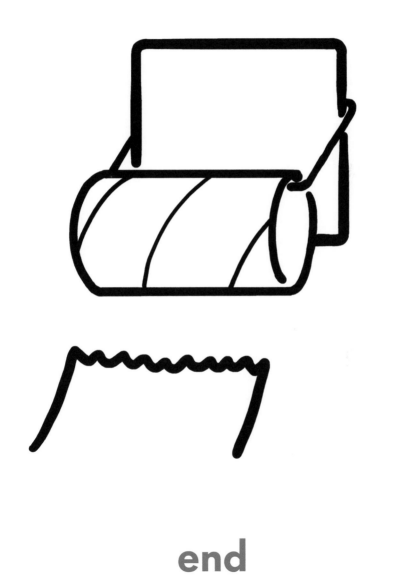

end

bat

bat

often

once

every

now

soon

some

scary

safe

kind

undecided

try

why

work

also

back

we

both

are

get

it

call

list

feel

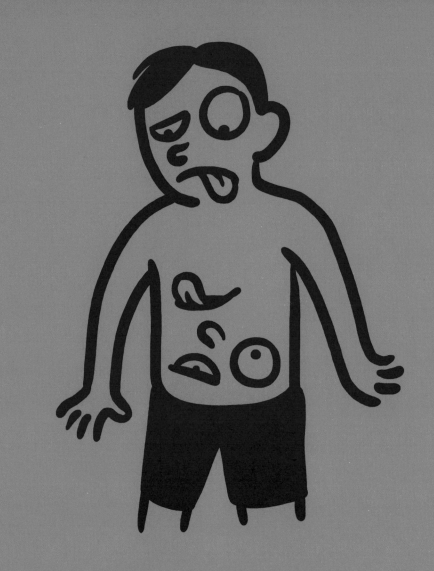

collywobbles

gobbledygook

man

boy

father

like

even

their

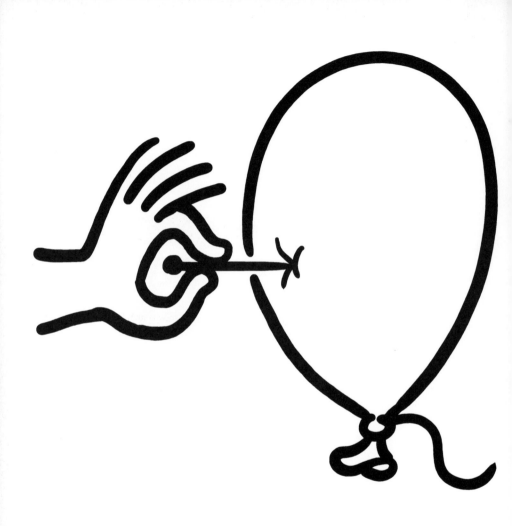

before

the

stay

play

sound

music

while

after

children

people

scintilla

Brobdingnagian

first

important

with

his

sometimes

sit

land

hill

mile

near

young

black

paper

she

her   **hair**

girl

were

an

apple

animal

plant

serve

food

which

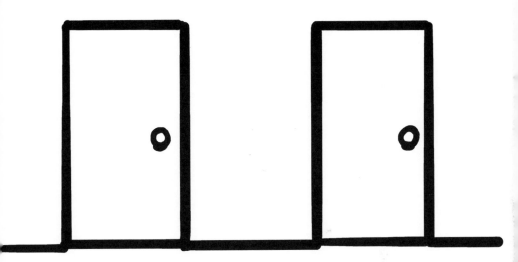

or

woebegone

effervescent

you

let's

be

different

how

learn

care

give

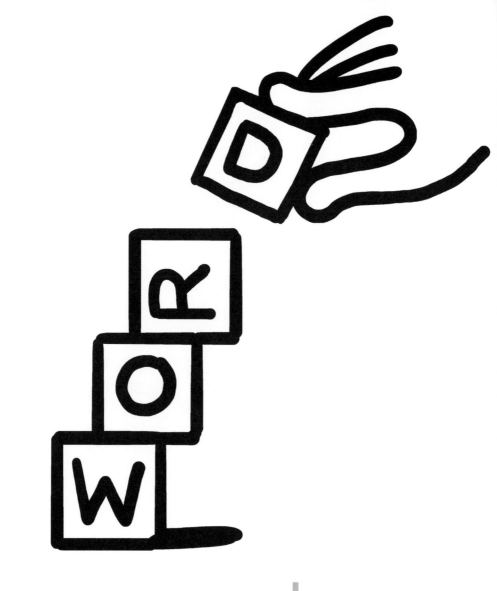

word

sentence

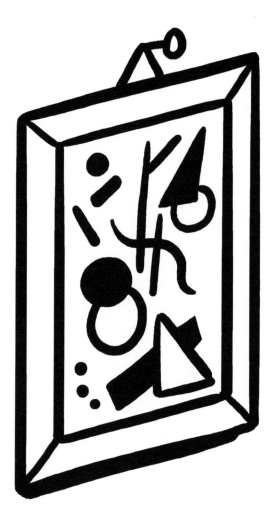

picture

look

use

study

know

live

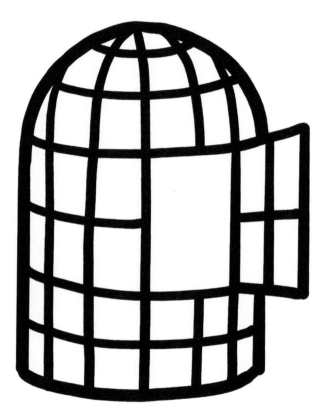

free

index

a 198
above 228
add 223
adjective 350
adverb 351
after 295
again 93–95
air 193
all 182
almost 17
along 185
also 271
always 54
an 318
and 166
animal 320
another 188
answer 190
any 154
apple 319
are 275
around 92
as 104
at 167
away 186

back 272
bad 45
bat 256, 257

be 330
been 108
before 288
begin 216
below 229
between 24
big 103
bird 63
black 312
book 205
both 274
bowl 96, 97
boy 283
Brobdingnagian 299
but 47
by 184

call 277
can 40
car 65
care 334
carry 149
cat 124
change 23
children 296
city 68
close 173
collywobbles 280
come 86
[comma] , 214
conjunction 351

could 34
country 69
cut 163

day 155
did 85
different 331
do 32
dog 62
dollop 160
don't 33
down 239
duck 18, 19

each 175
Earth 159
eat 136
effervescent 327
end 255
enough 48
even 286
every 260
example 127
[exclamation point] ! 39

fall 209
family 134
far 186
farm 135
father 284
fear 243

feel 279
feet 171
festooned 161
few 82
find 231
finger 172
first 300
five 81
flat 178, 179
follow 224
fond 221
food 323
for 129
four 80
free 344–45
from 164
full 213

get 276
girl 316
give 335
go 8
gobbledygook 281
good 37
got 210
great 203
group 133
grow 50

had 244
hair 315

half 83
hand 169
hard 254
has 206
have 130
he 236
head 170
hear 44
heavy 168
help 88
her 315
here 87
high 301
hill 308
him 89
his 304
home 72
hope 41
horse 140
house 67
how 332

I 9
idea 202
if 113
important 302
in 118
into 165
is 252
it 276

just 248

keep 220
kind 266
know 342

land 307
large 52
last 84
later 46
lean 234, 235
learn 333
leave 195
left 60
let's 329
letter 199
lickety-split 74
life 208
light 157
like 285
line 162
list 278
little 102
live 343
lollygag 196
long 110, 111
look 339
lost 230
love 16
low 51
luck 144

make 148
man 282
many 27
match 146, 147
me 232
might 138
mile 309
miss 55
more 143
most 28
mother 145
mountain 242
move 131
music 293
must 22
my 42

near 310
need 211
never 153
new 176
next 187
night 156
no 31
not 249
note 58, 59
noun 350
now 261
number 76

of 115
off 57
often 258
old 237
on 56
once 259
one 77
only 26
open 192
or 325
other 117
our 151
out 119
over 226
own 191

paper 313
part 132
pattern 247
people 297
[period] . 215
picture 338
plant 321
play 291
point 120
preposition 350
press 121
pronoun 350
put 10

[question mark] ? 38

read 212
real 53
rest 141
right 61
river 106
run 207

safe 265
said 245
scary 264
school 204
scintilla 298
sea 105
search 12
see 98
sentence 337
serve 322
set 222
share 142
she 314
ship 64
show 174
side 240
sit 306
sky 71
slowly 90
small 49

so 30
some 263
something 114
sometimes 305
somnambulist 197
song 43
soon 262
sound 292
spell 125
start 14
state 246
stay 290
stick 122, 123
still 109
stop 15
street 66
study 341

take 218
talk 250
tell 200
test 137
that 116
the 289
their 287
them 73
then 217
there 100
they 181

thing 219
think 13
this 128
those 101
thought 201
three 79
through 225
to 241
together 29
too 233
took 150
tree 107
try 268
turn 91
two 78

undecided 267
under 227
until 20
up 139
us 25
use 340

verb 351
very 253

want 126
was 194
watch 112

water 158
way 241
we 273
well 177
went 183
were 317
what 36
when 152
where 99
which 324
while 294
white 238
who 180
why 269
will 21
with 303
without 251
woebegone 326
wonky 75
word 336
work 270
world 70
would 35
write 11

year 189
you 328
young 311

noun   **adjective**

preposition   **pronoun**

verb **adverb**

conjunction

For Gustav

The author and the publisher gratefully acknowledge Lonni Tanner at SeeChangeNYC for her passion and expertise. This book originated as a joint project between SeeChangeNYC and the New York City Department of Education, and it was inspired in part by Dr. Edward Fry's list of sight words. Thank you as well to Julia Hoffmann and Susanne Vetter.

The images were drawn digitally in Adobe Photoshop.
The text type is 36-point Drescher Grotesk BT.

Library of Congress Cataloging-in-Publication Data is available.
ISBN 978-0-06-245550-5 (trade ed.)
"Greenwillow Books."
16 17 18 19 20 SCP 10 9 8 7 6 5 4 3 2 1
First Edition

GREENWILLOW BOOKS